The Magic Rabbit

RICHARD JESSE WATSON

THE BLUE SKY PRESS

An Imprint of Scholastic Inc. • *New York*

To Bonnie and Robbie
and
Chewie and Sniffy

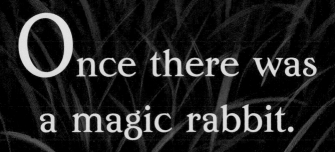

Once there was
a magic rabbit.

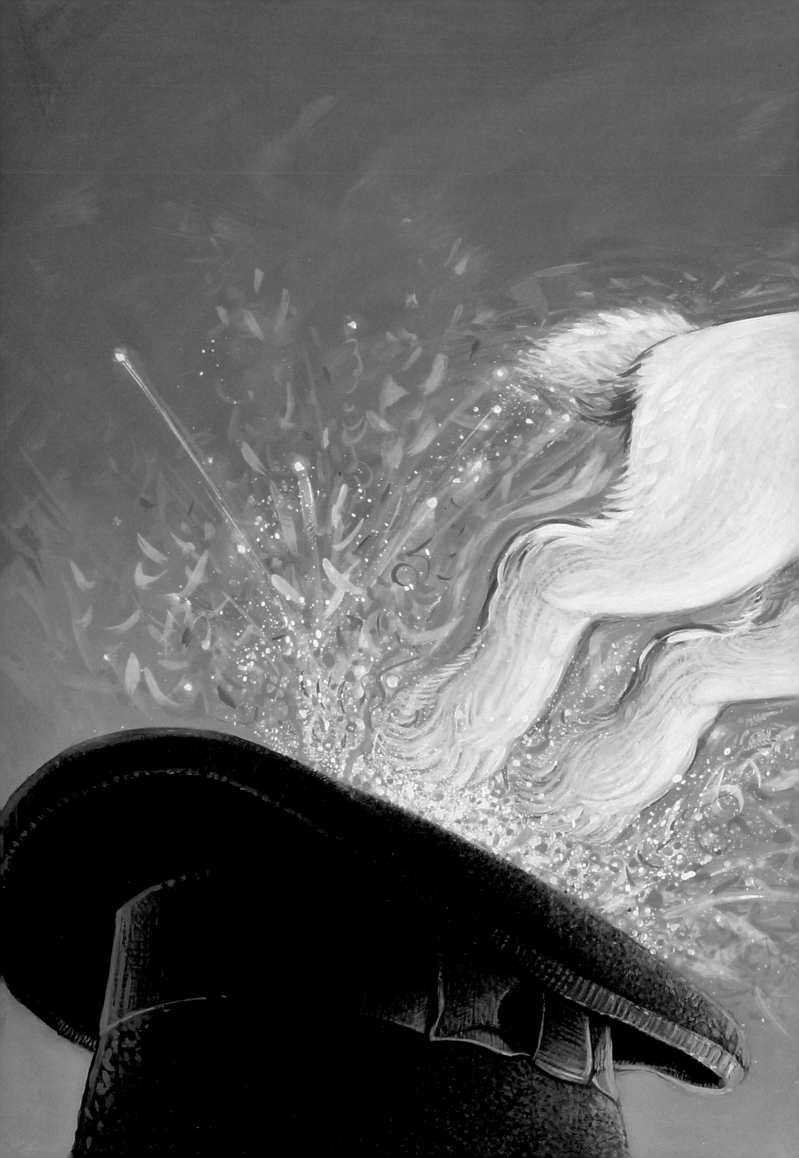

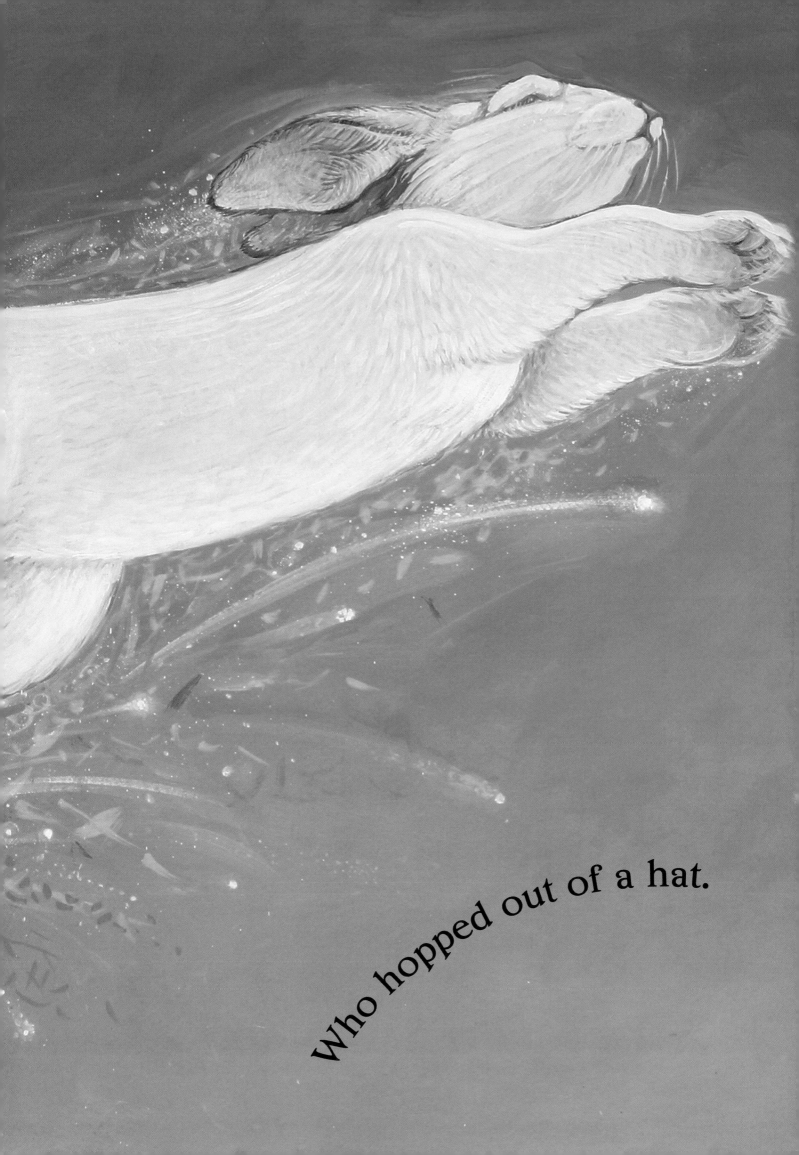

Who hopped out of a hat.

He found he
could do all

kinds of tricks
with the hat.

He could pull out balls and juggle them.

He could pull
out a scarf
that was tied

to another,

and another, and another . . .

VARROOM!

Beep! Beep!

Putt, putt, putt.

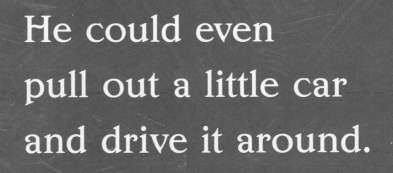

He could even
pull out a little car
and drive it around.

His yummiest trick was
making a picnic with
his favorite foods.

It was so
much fun,
except for
one thing:

He didn't have anyone
to share it with. "I
need a friend,"
he said.

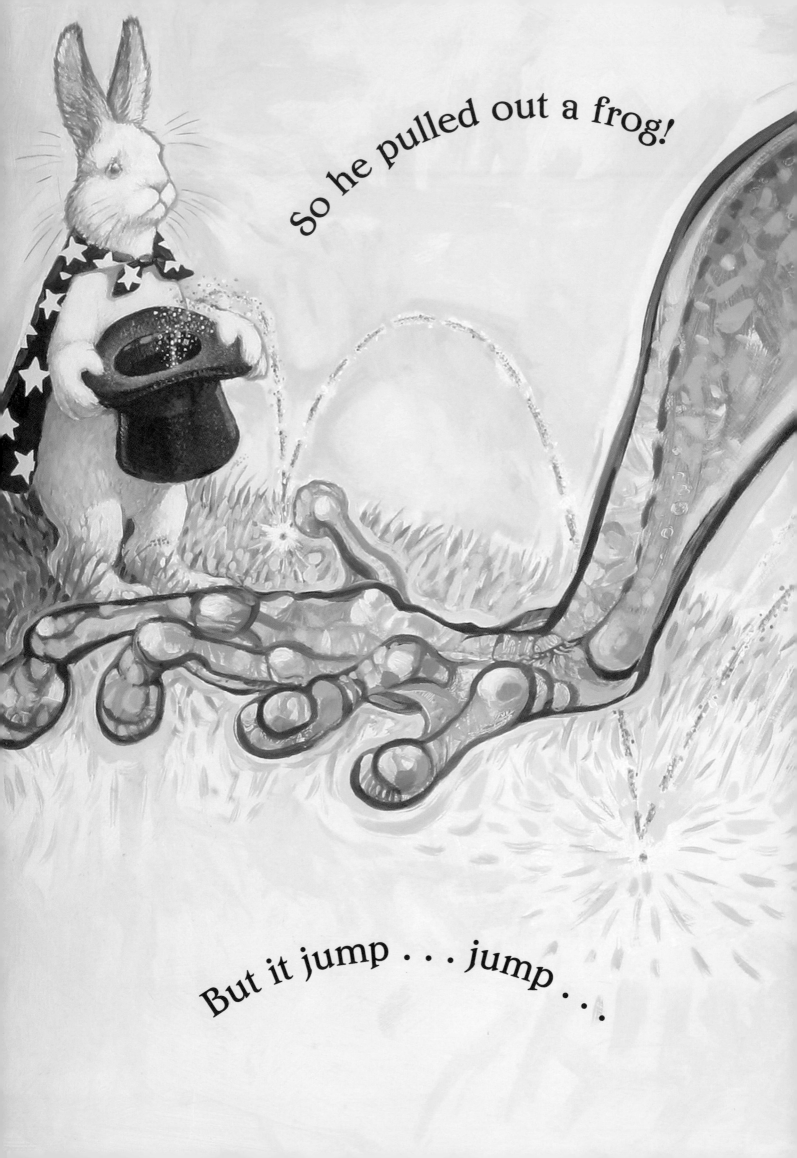

So he pulled out a frog!

But it jump . . . jump . . .

jumped away.

Next he pulled out

two mice,

but they scurry, scurry,
scurried away.

Then he pulled out a flutter of birds,

but they flap, flap, flew away.

"Oh dear," he said
with a sigh.

But then suddenly, he found
another hat
inside his
hat.

PRESTO!

Another magic rabbit
hopped out of
the new hat.

and the magic they shared.

But the best magic of all

was having a friend.

THE BLUE SKY PRESS

Copyright © 2005 by Richard Jesse Watson

For information regarding permission, please write to: Permissions Department,
Scholastic Inc., 557 Broadway, New York, New York 10012.

SCHOLASTIC, THE BLUE SKY PRESS, and associated logos are
trademarks and/or registered trademarks of Scholastic Inc.

Library of Congress catalog card number: 2004006383

ISBN 0-590-47964-4

10 9 8 7 6 5 4 3 2 1   05 06 07 08 09

Printed in Singapore   46

First printing, February 2005

The paintings in this book were executed in oil on Kapa®-Bloc.

Digital photography by Frank Ross Photographic

Designed by Kathleen Westray